It was Max's birthday.
He had a big party with chocolate cake.

1

He got lots of presents – pajamas from Uncle Frank,
a steam train from the Huffingtons
and three wind-up chicks from his sister, Ruby.

Beside the couch, Ruby found one gift that was still wrapped.
"Max! There's a present you forgot to open!" said Ruby.

Max stopped playing with the little yellow chicks.
He rushed over to see.

Ruby read the card.
"Happy Birthday, Max. From Aunt Claire and Uncle Nate."
Max couldn't wait to open his present.

"I wonder what it is?" said Ruby.
Max was so excited he ripped off all the wrapping paper
and tore open the box.

"It's a wind-up lobster. Say hello, Max," said Ruby.
Max didn't want to say hello. He was afraid of the lobster.
"No," he said.

The lobster climbed out of the box.
"It wants to play tag," said Ruby.
"No," said Max.

Max ran into the kitchen.
The lobster still wanted to play. It followed Max.

In the kitchen, Max played with his little yellow chicks.
He laughed as they splashed in the water.

The lobster wanted to play too.
"No," said Max.
The lobster would not stop. It knocked over the bowl.

Max had an idea. He ran outside.

The lobster still wanted to play. It followed Max.

Max ran back inside the house.
He closed the door and hid.

Ruby found Max hiding under the dining room table.
He had the last piece of chocolate birthday cake.

The lobster found Max there too.
Before Max could take one bite of the cake,
the lobster took it away.

"No," said Max.
The lobster would not stop. It crashed into the couch.
Cake flew everywhere.

Then the lobster chased Max around the kitchen table…

through the hallway…

and into the living room.

"Watch out for the box, Max!" warned Ruby.
But it was too late.

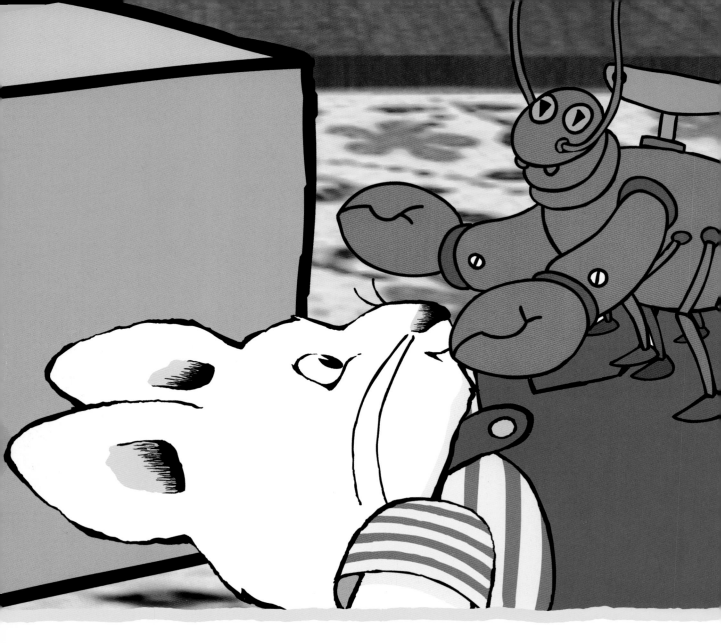

Max tripped over the box and fell onto his back.
The lobster climbed on top of Max.
Little lobster feet tickled Max's belly.

Ruby grabbed the wind-up toy.
"Let's put the lobster away,
so he won't scare you any more."

"No," said Max.
He took the lobster back from Ruby.
"Again!"